Mayo County Library
School Library Service

KV-684-156

Oh Auntie!

MAYO COUNTY LIBRARY
SCHOOL LIBRARY
SERVICE

Stephanie Dagg

Illustrated by Kim Shaw

MENTOR
BOOKS

J3

This Edition first published 2005 by

MENTOR BOOKS
43 Furze Road,
Sandyford Industrial Estate,
Dublin 18.
Tel. +353 1 295 2112/3   Fax. +353 1 295 2114
email: all@mentorbooks.ie

ISBN: 1-84210-332-6
A catalogue record for this book is available from the
British Library

Text copyright © Stephanie J Dagg 2005

The right of Stephanie Dagg to be identified as the Author
of the work has been asserted by her in accordance with the
Copyright Acts.

All rights reserved. No part of this publication may be
reproduced, stored in a retrieval system, or transmitted in
any form or by any means electronic, mechanical,
photocopying, recording, or otherwise, without prior written
permission of the publisher.

Illustrations: Kim Shaw
Editing, Design and Layout by Mentor Books

Printed in Ireland by ColourBooks Ltd.

1 3 5 7 9 10 8 6 4 2

Stephanie Dagg lives just outside Bandon, Co. Cork, with husband Chris and their three children Benjamin, Caitlín and Ruadhrí. They also have two dogs and some very spoilt chickens.

When she's not busy writing, Stephanie loves swimming and cycling, and doing arts and crafts.

Do visit Stephanie's websites at
www.booksarecool.com and
www.ecobabe.com.

Stephanie is committed to planting trees to contribute towards neutralising any carbon emisssions arising from publishing these books.

Contents

Dedicated to our

wonderful neighbours

and many great friends

here in Bandon

Chapter 1
Auntie's Here

'Auntie's here!' yelled Robyn as a sleek silver Porsche pulled into the farmyard. She had been watching out of the kitchen window with her younger brother Paul.

'At last!' sighed Dad. He and Mum were already late setting off. They were heading away to a big conference about organic farming, up in the city. And so Auntie had come to babysit for the weekend. Auntie was Mum's big sister. Her name was actually Jane but she'd never liked that, so she kept changing it. Over the years she had been Jade, Joy, Janet, Janine, Jemima, Jaime, Jasmine, Jackie, Judy, Jontie and Jennifer. It was very confusing so that was why everyone, even Mum and Dad, just called her Auntie.

Auntie had an important job in the city and was very rich. She drove fast cars and had a huge wardrobe of designer label clothes. She was tall, elegant and beautiful. But she wasn't much fun. Robyn and Paul were reckoning on having a very boring weekend with her.

Auntie got out of her car and picked her way carefully across the muddy farmyard in her high stiletto shoes. She was wearing a Ralph Lauren lilac trouser suit and a matching Deva pashmina with glittering crystals on the tassles. She shimmered into the kitchen. Mum gave her a hug. Auntie winced.

'Don't crumple my suit, there's a dear,' she said, smoothing imaginary crinkles out of the fabric. George, run and get my suitcases. And don't scratch the car.'

Oh Auntie!

Dad went outside grumbling. He didn't like Auntie much. She was very bossy. It took three trips to bring all Auntie's matching Burberry suitcases and bags into the guest room.

'Goodness, whatever's all that for? You're only here for a couple of days!' laughed Mum as Dad staggered by with the last of the luggage.

Auntie glared at her. 'I assure you, it's all essential.'

Mum shrugged and winked at the children. 'Right, we need to go. Be good for Auntie please.'

'And do keep an eye on Barbie,' said Dad. 'She shouldn't calve just yet, but if she does, tell Billy at once. OK?'

Robyn and Paul nodded wearily. Dad had told them what to do at least fifty times already that day. But Barbie – named by Robyn when she was a little girl – was his favourite cow and Dad was a bit of a worrier. Billy was the farmhand and he lived just down the road.

'Time we went!' said Mum.

And after lots of kisses and hugs and more sets of instructions from Dad they drove away in their old but reliable jeep.

Chapter 2
Auntie Unpacks

Auntie began to unpack her suitcases. Robyn and Paul tried to slink off but Auntie summoned them back.

'Take this to the kitchen,' she commanded Robyn, handing her a silver machine of some kind that was all levers and dials. 'And don't drop it.'

That was hard – it weighed a tonne! 'What is it?' gasped Robyn.

'My espresso machine,' explained Auntie. 'I'm very fussy about my coffee. Paul, you take these.'

She handed him an assortment of tins and packets of vegetables.

'Why have you brought veggies?' he asked amazed. 'The freezer is stuffed full with ones we grow on the farm.'

'I'm very fussy about my vegetables,' replied Auntie with a sniff.

The children tottered to the kitchen with their loads.

'She never once says "please",' moaned Robyn, putting the heavy espresso machine down gratefully.

'Or "thank you",' grumbled Paul, dumping his load on the counter.

'How on earth can she and Mum be related?' asked Robyn. 'I mean, Mum's so nice and normal and, well, Auntie isn't.'

MAYO COUNTY LIBRARY
SCHOOL LIBRARY
SERVICE

'True, but she has a wicked car. I'm going to have a proper look at it!' And with that Paul dashed out of the kitchen.

'Come back!' yelled Robyn, but Paul ignored her. So while he drooled over the Porsche for the next half hour, poor Robyn ran backwards and forwards with all Auntie's bits and pieces. There were half a dozen bottles of spring water, a juicer, a smoothie maker, three packets of different sorts of coffee beans, lots of jars of vitamin pills, and plenty of tins of fancy-looking food.

Robyn was soon exhausted. Meanwhile Auntie had started checking for emails on her laptop computer.

'Now run along while I get changed,' ordered Auntie. 'I suppose I'd better have a look at this horrible, dirty farm of yours.'

Robyn hurried away thankfully. What a rotten weekend this was going to be.

Chapter 3
Farm Walk

B ut Robyn soon cheered up when Auntie finally emerged from the farmhouse.

'Oh Auntie!' she chuckled.

She couldn't help laughing! Auntie's idea of a suitable outfit consisted of a gold Ralph Lauren silk blouse, a black Spanish bolero, Armani bootleg jeans, real snakeskin cowboy boots with enormous heels and a huge cowboy hat. Auntie would have looked great on the catwalk – but she looked plain silly on a farm walk. Paul snorted merrily when he saw her.

'Shut up!' hissed Robyn as Auntie approached, digging him firmly in the ribs.

'Let's make this quick,' snapped Auntie. 'The feng shui is all wrong out here. It will drain me of energy.'

'Feng what?' whispered Paul.

'Feng shui,' Robyn informed him. 'It's a Chinese idea about having everything in the right place. It's bad for you if it isn't.'

'But everything is in the right place here!'

16

protested Paul. 'I mean, the tractor's in the tractor shed and the hens are in the henhouse and the pigs are in the pigsty and …'

'It's a bit more complicated than that,' said Robyn. 'Don't worry about it.'

'OK,' shrugged Paul. And he didn't.

'Come and see the lambs, Auntie,' suggested Robyn brightly.

'If I must,' grimaced Auntie.

As she followed the children towards the field, she pulled out her mobile phone and began making calls. She hardly bothered looking at the frisky little lambs. She wasn't interested in the pigs or the cows either. And Mum's flock of fancy Silkie chickens left her cold. She just barked orders into her phone the whole time and looked disapproving.

'Are we done yet?' she asked in a bored voice, in between calls.

'I guess,' shrugged Paul.

'Not quite,' Robyn corrected her brother. He looked at her puzzled. They'd seen all the animals now. 'Come and see where we've planted our pumpkins for Halloween.'

Paul stared at his sister as though she were mad. They'd put the seeds in only the day before. There was nothing to see at all, only a patch of bare ground. But Robyn winked at him, and he grinned. He knew what she was up to now! The only way to get to their pumpkin patch was along the muddy, churned-up path that the cows took to get from the field to the milking parlour.

'Oh Auntie, please!' begged Paul, giving her a wide-eyed, beseeching look.

'All right, but then straight back to the house,' agreed Auntie reluctantly.

So the children squelched happily along the path. Auntie slipped and slid behind them, muttering crossly. She had to stop making calls so she could concentrate on not falling over. Only she didn't concentrate hard enough. A sudden, boggy patch took her by surprise. She lost her balance and plunged face first into the soft, gloopy mud. Her phone flew out of her hand and disappeared into a deep, slimy puddle.

The children watched in horrified silence as a bog monster rose up from the ground in front of them. It dripped. It oozed. It slurped. Then it screamed out: 'FIND MY PHONE!' Finally it turned and fled towards the house.

Robyn and Paul looked at each other – and burst into gales of laughter. They hadn't meant Auntie to fall in the mud but they were quite glad she had!

'Oh Auntie!' they giggled.

SCHOOL LIBRARY SERVICE

Chapter 4

Where Do Eggs Come From?

S0027049

It hadn't taken them long to find Auntie's phone. Within seconds of her storming off, it had begun to beep frantically, none the worse for being dunked in a muddy puddle. So they'd scooped it out, given it a quick rinse under the outside tap and left it in the kitchen sink to drip-dry.

It was two hours before Auntie emerged from the bathroom, clean but furious. Robyn and Paul spent the time in the cow shed with Billy, doing odd jobs and keeping an eye on Barbie.

'I'm hungry,' said Paul suddenly.

'Me too,' agreed Robyn. 'Come on, we'll have to go back to the house.'

They slipped in quietly. The kitchen

SCHOOL LIBRARY SERVICE

smelt of very strong coffee. Paul wrinkled his nose in disgust. Auntie was standing at her espresso machine, pushing one of the levers with one hand, and talking into her still slightly muddy phone which she was holding with the other. She was wearing a long, flowing Versace dressing gown.

'I suppose you two want feeding,' she snapped icily, when the call ended.

'Yes please!' said Paul greedily.

'It's all right, I can make us sandwiches,' offered Robyn.

'No, I promised my sister I'd look after you so that's what I'll do,' replied Auntie. 'What would you like? Some ghastly greasy food I suppose.'

'No thanks,' smiled Robyn. 'We would like scrambled eggs on toast please.' That was her brother's favourite snack.

'Yum!' said Paul.

'Very well,' said Auntie.

There was a loaf of Mum's homemade bread in the bread bin. Mum's bread had lots of intesting bits in it.

'Good gracious,' exclaimed Auntie, picking it up and inspecting it with a sneer. 'What does your mother use to make it with? Sawdust and fir cones?'

'Wholemeal granary flour actually,' Robyn told her primly.

'And where are the eggs? I can't see any,' snapped Auntie.

'Oh! That's because we forgot to collect them,' admitted Robyn. 'Come on Paul.'

They charged off with the basket to the henhouse and were soon back with a good harvest of eggs. Auntie examined them.

'This one's all lumpy,' she protested.

'Britney's eggs are always like that,' said Paul.

'This one is huge!'

'That's probably Avril's then,' Robyn told her.

'And this one is a very wonky shape.'

'That's Kylie's,' replied Robyn and Paul together.

'Are all your chickens named after popstars?' asked Auntie.

'Pretty much,' nodded Robyn.

'The rooster is called McFly,' Paul informed her.

Auntie tut-tutted and picked up another egg. 'This is a very muddy one,' she moaned. 'In fact, lots of them are muddy.'

'That's not mud,' piped up Paul. 'That's chicken poop. Well, they do come out of a chicken's . . .'

'Eek!' screamed Auntie, throwing the egg in the air. Robyn caught it.

'Oh Auntie!' she sighed. 'All you have to do is wipe them clean. There's no need to make such a fuss.'

Chapter 5
Barbie

The rest of the day didn't go too badly. Auntie spent most of the time on her computer while Robyn and Paul played outside. There was some excitement when they caught sight of a fox in one of the fields. They rushed in to tell Auntie and ask if she wanted to see it.

'No thank you,' she said coldly. 'Why don't you get Billy to shoot it?'

'What for?' Paul wanted to know.

'I thought that's what country people did,' shrugged Auntie. 'Nasty vermin, foxes.' She shuddered.

'Actually, under the Wildlife Act they're not vermin,' Robyn said crossly. 'It's just stupid people who think they are.'

Auntie ignored the dig. 'But won't they eat your chickens?' she asked.

'Only if we don't shut them away at night,' said Paul.

'Come on, let's go,' muttered Robyn, furious at Auntie. 'Honestly, she doesn't know anything!'

They went to check on Barbie who seemed a bit restless.

'I bet it's because of Auntie,' declared Paul. 'All the animals know how horrid she is and it's upsetting them.'

Robyn nodded in agreement.

They stayed in the cowshed the rest of the day, only going back into the house for tea. Auntie steamed a huge array of exotic vegetables for herself and did sausages and beans for the children. They finished off with one of Mum's yummy blackberry crumbles out of the freezer. Even Auntie ate some.

Auntie sent them to bed a good bit earlier than usual. Probably it had something to do with the muddy path episode. Paul grumbled in protest, but Robyn just shrugged. She had no intention of staying in bed. She planned to sneak out later and watch Barbie. Billy the farmhand was going out tonight she knew, so she thought she had better keep an eye on the cow.

As soon as Robyn heard the television going on, she tiptoed down the stairs and out through the kitchen door. She could hear Barbie mooing as soon as she got outside.

'Uh oh!' she cried.

And sure enough Barbie looked very stressed. She was clearly in pain.

Robyn charged back to the house and threw pebbles at Paul's window. One pebble was rather large and a small crack appeared on the window pane.

'Oh rats!' thought Robyn.

Then Paul's face appeared. Robyn gestured at him frantically to come down. A minute later he was in the cowshed with her.

'What shall we do?' he asked, looking at Barbie. 'Call a vet?'

'Go and see if Jim is in,' decided Robyn. Jim was their neighbour and he was also a farmer. 'I'll stay with Barbie. Cut across the fields, Paul. That way you won't have to go on the road. Take this torch.'

She unhooked the emergency torch Dad kept hung on a nail in the cowshed and gave it to him. He shot off. Robyn stroked poor Barbie's nose and whispered her name, trying to calm the animal down.

'Hurry, hurry!' she begged her brother.

And he did. Barely ten minutes later Robyn heard footsteps, and Jim and Paul ran into the barn.

'Right, let's see what's going on inside,' Jim said, quickly washing his arm under the tap in the cowshed. 'Looks like the calf is lying awkwardly. I'll soon deal with that.'

In the house, Auntie suddenly noticed lights on in the cowshed when she came out of the bathroom.

'Those stupid, naughty children!' she exclaimed, and stormed outside, pausing only to pull on her Versace dressing gown and matching turban.

She bustled angrily into the cowshed. The children jumped. Auntie jumped too, startled by the scene before her. It was a few seconds before she recovered.

'Why has this stranger got his arm inside your cow?' she gasped, going very green.

'And why have you got bandages on your head?' asked Paul, puzzled. 'And this is not a stranger, it's Jim.'

Jim waved with his free hand.

'Hi! I'm a neighbour!' he smiled. 'Just sorting out a spot of bother.'

'Well, you're obviously in control so

Oh Auntie!

I'll leave you to it,' said Auntie gratefully, turning to leave. Unfortunately she rested her hand just a little bit too long on one of the calf pens on her way. The grey nose of a Brown Swiss calf appeared through the bars, and a rough, slurpy, black tongue quickly wound itself round her fingers. Auntie screamed as she felt them sucked into the calf's mouth with a very strong suck indeed.

'Eek!' shrieked Auntie. 'Get it off me!'

Robyn and Paul burst out laughing. Jim's mouth twitched too.

'It's biting me!' screeched Auntie, feeling something rough on her hand.

'Oh Auntie!' chuckled Robyn, coming to the rescue. 'Don't be silly. He's only got a few tiny bottom teeth. Now then Gareth, let go of Auntie.'

Robyn tickled the calf's nose and at once he began sucking on her fingers instead.

Auntie stifled a sob as she looked at the soggy, slobbery cuff of her Versace dressing gown and then scampered back to the house as fast as she could.

The children were still giggling five minutes later when Jim carefully eased Barbie's calf out of her and onto the waiting straw.

'Brill! A heifer, Dad will be pleased!' gasped Paul.

'Yes, she's gorgeous!' sighed Robyn. 'Thanks Jim.'

'You're very welcome,' said Jim. 'So, kids, tell me a bit about that glamorous Auntie of yours while I clean up.'

'Whatever do you want to know about Auntie for?' wondered Paul.

But Robyn was already telling Jim everything!

Chapter 6
Tractor Ride

Next day they were all up late, the children because they'd been out in the cowshed until after midnight with Barbie and the new calf, and Auntie because the noisy countryside had kept her awake for hours. There had been owls hooting and foxes barking and cows mooing and leaves rustling in the wind. Auntie had longed for the soothing hum of city traffic to lull her to sleep.

But when she got up, she was quite jolly. She made them all smoothies in her special machine.

'Wow, these are really nice!' Robyn exclaimed. 'I'll ask Mum to make them sometimes.'

'They're very easy,' said Auntie, 'and very healthy.'

'Is coffee healthy?' asked Paul. Auntie was on her third teeny tiny cup of espresso already.

'Well . . . no,' admitted Auntie, 'but life's not worth living without coffee.'

Paul nodded wisely. 'I know what you mean,' he said. 'I'm the same about jelly beans, especially the black ones.'

'What shall we do today?' asked Robyn.

'We'll go for a walk,' said Auntie. 'I always go for a walk on Sunday mornings. But along roads,' she added firmly.

So half an hour later they set off along the lane. It went steeply uphill for a while. Paul and Robyn trudged along in jumpers, jeans and wellies while Auntie had gone for a Bohemian look. She was wearing a frilly, billowing, ankle-length Gucci dress and she clipped along in some fragile,

strappy Via Spiga sandals with high heels. She looked tremendous but frozen.

'Are those shoes comfy?' Robyn couldn't help asking.

'I could walk around the world in these,' Auntie replied. 'They cost me a fortune but they're worth every cent.'

At the top of the hill they turned right towards the village. They passed one of Jim's fields. He was driving his tractor and trimming the hedges. It was a poor field and sloped very steeply, especially in the far corner.

'Goodness, that tractor is really tilting,' gasped Auntie. 'It won't roll over will it?'

'No,' said Robyn firmly. But that very second, Jim turned a bit too sharply on the slope. The three of them watched in horror as the tractor suddenly began to topple. It fell with a crash onto the hedgerow that Jim had been trimming. It was stuck at a steep angle, lying on its side where the door was. Jim wasn't hurt but he was stuck inside.

'Quick! We must call an ambulance and the fire brigade!' cried Auntie. 'And I've left my phone at home. Oh no!'

'It's OK,' soothed Robyn. 'We'll be

able to drag him out with our tractor. Paul, go and tell Jim we'll rescue him. I'll go and find Billy!'

Paul set off down the field and Robyn turned and ran back to the farm. Auntie hitched up her dress and trotted after her as quickly as her high heels would let her.

But Robyn couldn't find the farmhand anywhere. She was breathless from all the dashing around when Auntie finally caught up with her at the farm.

'He must have gone to church,' gasped Robyn. 'He won't be back for an hour.'

'We can't leave Jim stuck for that long,' said Auntie firmly. 'Where's your tractor? I'll go and rescue him myself.'

'The John Deere's in the shed behind the barn,' said Robyn, 'but Auntie, I'm not sure you'll be able to drive it.'

'Of course I will,' snapped Auntie, striding off. 'A tractor's just like a big car, isn't it?'

'Um, not really,' Robyn told her.

And Robyn was right. When Auntie clambered into the tractor cab she had a bit of a shock. There were two gear sticks for a start and the pedals weren't in a neat row like in a car. There were two on the right side and one on the left. And there was a long row of switches above the windscreen.

But Auntie wasn't put off easily. She turned the key and the engine rumbled into life. She stamped down on what she hoped was the clutch and wiggled one of the gearsticks around. There was an awful grating sound. Robyn, who was watching her from the shed doorway, winced.

'Oops, wrong one,' gulped Auntie and tried the other gearstick. This time when she eased her foot up, the tractor lurched backwards into the shed wall with a crunch. After a bit more gearstick wiggling and more awful groans from the engine, Auntie finally managed to get the tractor moving the right way. Robyn leapt out of its path as it swerved out of the shed.

'Get a rope,' screeched Auntie out of the cab, 'and follow me.'

So as the tractor wove its way drunkenly through the yard and trundled jerkily down the drive, Robyn zoomed to the garage where Dad kept a strong tow rope. Just as she reached the door, there was a horrible crunch as Auntie knocked down the gatepost at the farm entrance.

'Oh Auntie!' Robyn sighed. 'Dad will go nuts!'

Robyn dragged the rope off its hook, looped it over her shoulder and jumped on her bike. She pedalled up the hill behind the tractor as it veered crazily this way and that along the road.

It was a scary journey for Auntie up in the tractor cab. She didn't like being so high up and she was still struggling with the gears and the steering. She was very glad when she saw the entrance to Jim's field ahead. She swung in sharply, taking down a small fence post, and began to career down the hilly field. Paul and Jim watched in horror as the tractor bore down on them. But at the last moment, Auntie found the brake and slowed right down and began to pull in neatly behind Jim's tractor, ready to tow him out of the ditch.

'Oh Auntie, well done!' cheered Paul.

But he spoke too soon. Instead of putting the tractor into neutral before she stopped, Auntie cranked the gearstick into reverse by mistake. The tractor plunged backwards. In a panic Auntie plonked her foot on the accelerator instead of the brake. With a grinding crunch she crashed into Jim's tractor. Now both tractors were toppled over in the corner of the field.

Robyn came running down the field. She'd left her bike at the gate.

'Oh Auntie!' she groaned. 'Now what will we do?'

Chapter 7
Farmer Auntie

Two hours later, they were all back home. Robyn had cycled to the church and had been waiting for Billy outside with all the news.

The farmhand had rescued both Jim and Auntie eventually. He'd used Dad's other tractor to tow them both to safety.

'What a nice man that Jim is,' said Auntie after her second espresso.

'Yes, we all like him,' said Paul.

'He said I was very brave to try and rescue him in the tractor, seeing as how I'd never driven one before,' she smiled.

Brave wasn't the word Robyn would have used.

'And he liked my outfit,' she glowed.

'He said it was elegant.'

Elegant wasn't the word Paul would have used.

'Now, who babysits for you when I'm not around? Jim wants to take me out to dinner tonight to say "thank you" for rescuing him,' Auntie told them.

That didn't seem fair. For a start Billy had actually rescued Jim. And then it had been Robyn who'd thought of using the tractor in the first place and who'd also advised Auntie not to drive it. It had been Robyn who'd hauled the heavy tow rope on her bike all the way from the farm. And it had been Robyn who'd cycled all the way to the church to get Billy. Robyn had done all the hard work. All Auntie had done was drive the tractor and bash into things!

'Who knows,' smiled Auntie coyly. 'Maybe I'll be a farmer's wife one day.'

Robyn and Paul stared at her in disbelief. No way would Auntie last five minutes living on a farm full-time! But if by any awful, remote chance she did end up as Mrs Jim next door, they would definitely run away from home.

'I actually think I'd be very good at it,' Auntie went on, 'now that I know to keep away from muddy paths, and free range chicken eggs, and calves, and tractors – oh, yes and not shoot foxes.'

Robyn and Paul grinned. Auntie was learning fast.

'Oh Auntie!' they laughed.

'So,' mused Auntie. 'What shall I wear?

MAYO COUNTY LIBRARY
SCHOOL LIBRARY SERVICE

MORE BOOKS FROM THE *OH!* SERIES

Santa is still worn out after last Christmas, so Teddy Bear Jake decides it's time to get Santa fit. But will Christmas be the same with a slimmer, super-fit Santa?